CRANKY PAWS

PET VET

Book #1 CRANKY PAWS

Book #2 THE MARE'S TALE

Book #3 MOTORBIKE BOB

Book #4 THE PYTHON PROBLEM

Book #5 THE KITTEN'S TALE

Book #6 THE PUP'S TALE

First American Edition 2009
by Kane/Miller Book Publishers, Inc.
La Jolla, California

First published by Scholastic Australia in 2008.
Text copyright © Sally and Darrel Odgers, 2008.
Illustrations copyright © Janine Dawson, 2008.
Cover copyright © Scholastic, 2008.
Cover design by Natalie Winter.

Library of Congress Control Number: 2008933430
Printed and bound in the United States of America
16 17 18 19 20 21

ISBN: 978-1-935279-01-3

CRANKY PAWS

Darrel & Sally Odgers

Illustrated By Janine Dawson

Kane Miller
A DIVISION OF EDC PUBLISHING

Welcome to Pet Vet Clinic!

My name is Trump, and Pet Vet Clinic is where I live and work.

At Pet Vet, Dr. Jeanie looks after sick or hurt animals from the town of Cowfork as well as the animals that live at nearby farms and stables.

I live with Dr. Jeanie in Cowfork House, which is attached to the clinic. Smaller animals come to Pet

Vet for treatment. If they are very sick, or if they need operations, they stay for a day or more in the hospital ward which is at the clinic.

In the morning, Dr. Jeanie drives out on her rounds, visiting farm animals that are too big to be brought to the clinic. We see the smaller patients in the afternoons.

It's hard work, but we love it. Dr. Jeanie says that helping animals and their people is the best job in the world.

Staff at the Pet Vet Clinic

Dr. Jeanie: The vet who lives at Cowfork House and runs Pet Vet Clinic.

Trump: Me! Dr. Jeanie's Animal Liaison Officer, and a Jack Russell terrier.

Davie Raymond: The Saturday helper.

Other Important Characters

Dr. Max: Dr. Jeanie's grandfather. The retired owner of Pet Vet Clinic.

Major Higgins: The visiting cat. If  he doesn't know something, he can soon find out.

Whiskey: Dr. Max's cockatoo.

Patients

Cranky Paws: A mysterious patient at Pet Vet Clinic.

Map of Pet Vet Clinic

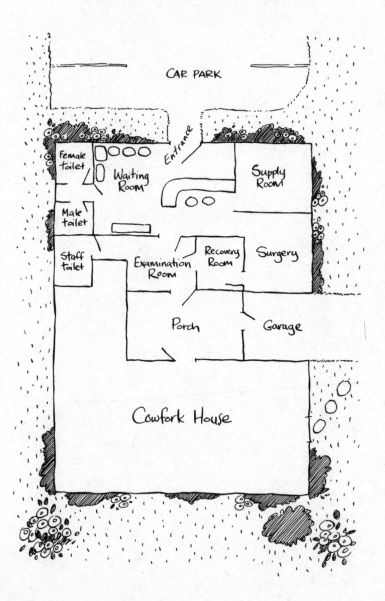

The Beginning of Things

All the patients that come to Pet **Vet** Clinic are interesting, but some are more interesting than others.

Take Cranky Paws the cat, for example ...

Her name wasn't really Cranky Paws, but that's what Dr. Jeanie and I called

> **Vet** or **Veterinarian** (vet-er-in-AIR-ee-an) – A doctor who treats animals.

her. I'd never met a cat who was so determined to hate everyone!

❖

Cranky Paws came into our lives soon after we moved into Cowfork House. Dr. Jeanie had just finished her training at Jeandabah **Veterinary College**.

> **Veterinary College** – A special school where vets are trained.

She took over at Pet Vet because Dr. Max, her grandfather, wanted to retire.

Dr. Max helped Dr. Jeanie to learn her routine. His **cockatoo**, Whiskey, did the same thing for me.

On our very first day, Dr. Jeanie and Dr. Max drove out in the Pet Vet van to visit a sick cow. They left Whiskey and me behind at Cowfork House.

> **Cockatoo** (COCK-a-too) – Any parrot that has a crest of feathers on its head.

As soon as the van had gone, Whiskey undid his cage bolt with his beak and climbed onto the top. He looked down at me. I looked up at him. I don't know what *he* was thinking, but *I* was wondering if I could reach up to tweak his tail.

"Don't even think about it, dog," said Whiskey.

I pricked up my ears. He was talking like a human. I'd heard him do that before, but he'd been squawking about biscuits then.

9

"Don't stare, dog," said Whiskey. "Time's a'wasting, and there's a lot to learn."

I cocked my head to one side. "I've got lots of time. I'm going to sniff-sniff around the yard and then dig for bones under the back step."

I didn't expect Whiskey to understand me. Animals speak their own languages, just like humans. Dogs and cats understand some Human-speak (which is why I had understood Whiskey), but you won't often see a rabbit talking to a hen.

Whiskey did understand, though. He answered me right away, and what's more, he did it in Dog-speak. "Forget bones and steps, dog," he said. "And don't even *think* about tweaking my tail feathers. If you're going to be a good A.L.O., you have to get started *now*."

"What's an A.L.O.?" I asked.

Whiskey flapped his wings.

"An A.L.O. is an Animal **Liaison**

> **Liaison Officer**
> (Lee-AZE-n
> off-iss-er) –
> Someone who
> helps explain
> things and
> makes sure two
> different groups
> understand each
> other.

Officer," he said. "Only very lucky vets have one. You want your Dr. Jeanie to feel lucky, don't you?"

"But I don't know what an Animal Liaison Officer is! Mum and Dad never taught me about that."

Whiskey scratched his crest with a claw. "An Animal Liaison Officer is an animal who acts as go-between between animals with problems and the humans who want to help them. Get it?"

I liked the sound of being a go-between. "Good!" I said. "Terriers do a lot of going between toys and bones and food and friends and –"

Whiskey flapped his wings again. "Enough! You have a lot to learn, dog, and I'm the cockatoo to make it happen. Pay attention. Stop looking at my tail."

"I am a terrier," I explained. "Terriers notice everything. We chase things that move, and we bark at things that don't. We dig, and we leap and we seek. That's all part of what we do and what we are."

"You have to learn to be an A.L.O. first and a dog second," said Whiskey. "Noticing is good for an A.L.O. Chasing is bad. Save your digging for your days off. And *stop* looking at my tail." He leaned right down so his beak was close to my nose. It was grey and curved, and it looked as if it could give a nasty nip. I backed away.

"You are not a pet dog when you are on duty, Trump," said Whiskey sternly. "You are an A.L.O. Being an A.L.O. is a noble calling. Get it?"

"Got it!" I liked the idea of being noble.

"You must learn to talk to other animals," said Whiskey, hoisting himself back onto the top of the cage.

"I can't do that!" I protested. "Dad told me dogs can only talk to dogs. Cats can only talk to cats. Cockatoos can only talk to –"

"Cockatoos talk to everyone," stated Whiskey. "Being a dog, it will be harder for you, but you must learn this if you're going to be an A.L.O. You'll have to learn fast, because Dr. Max and I will soon be going on a holiday."

Anything a bird can do, a terrier can do better, apart from flying, of course. I made up my mind I was going to be the best Animal Liaison Officer a vet had ever had. Dr. Jeanie deserves the very best.

"I will learn," I said.

"Right!" said Whiskey. "We'll start by introducing you to Major Higgins. He can give you a lesson on Cat-speak …"

Chapter 2

Diagnosing Dodger

By the time Dr. Max and Whiskey
went on their holiday, I had learned
to be an A.L.O.

My main duty was acting as a
go-between for animal patients
and helpful humans, especially
Dr. Jeanie. When animals are sick,
Dr. Jeanie explains things to their
people, and I explain things to the
animals themselves. It isn't easy.
Have *you* ever tried to tell a dog
with stitches that he must *not* chew

at them? Have you ever tried to tell a cat it must swallow something horrible so it can get well?

Sometimes, I get Distress Calls from animals that need my help or advice. Dogs send the most calls, because they have loud barks to pass on information. If it's a cat in trouble, Major Higgins sometimes brings the message. (You'll meet Major Higgins later in this chapter.)

One morning a Distress Call came just as Davie Raymond, our Saturday helper, arrived at Pet Vet Clinic. Davie is my friend, but I stay out of the way on Saturday mornings when he is doing the cleaning. The smell of **disinfectant** makes me sneeze.

The call came from Dodger, who

Disinfectant
(dis-in-FECT-nt)
– Chemical for killing germs.

lives with Cordelia Applebloom. I wasn't surprised to hear from him. Dodger is a healthy border collie, but he often gets sick. Why? Because he eats anything, whether it's good for him or not. He goes anywhere, whether it's safe or not. He runs up to anyone, whether they like him or not. He's the kind of dog who acts first then thinks later. His favorite word is "oops!"

I nosed Dr. Jeanie's leg to let her know I was going out, and set off.

When I got to Dodger's place, he was scratching and groaning. I let myself into his yard, and trotted up to the kennel. It's a fancy one with a nameplate on the side.

"What's the problem, Dodger?"

Dodger groaned, and stuck his nose out. "Help me, Trump! I've got an awful itch. It hurts."

"Show me," I said.

Dodger crept out of the kennel. Then he sat down and scratched at his neck. "Owwww," he said. "There."

I sniffed him cautiously. He had scratched a sore spot on the back of his neck. I could see another place on his flank where the skin was red and inflamed.

"It's so itchy!" groaned Dodger.

"I'm not surprised," I said. "I **diagnose** a nasty case of fleas."

"I can't have fleas," objected Dodger. "Cordelia gave me a bath last week."

As Dr. Jeanie says, there is no point in making a diagnosis

Diagnose (die-ag-NOSE) – Identify a problem or sickness.

if you're not prepared to follow
it with **sound direction**, so I gave
Dodger sound
direction.

> **Sound direction**
> – Good advice.

"Cordelia
used rose-scented soap when she
bathed you," I said. "She should use
flea soap instead."

"I hate flea soap," whined Dodger.

"So do fleas," I said. "Do you
want your fleas dead, or alive and
smelling like roses? Cordelia should
wash your bedding, too. There's no
point in getting you flea-free if you
have a flea-farm in your kennel."

"But what can *I* do?" cried Dodger.

"Show Cordelia what you need.
Scratch yourself in front of her. Roll
on your back and show her your

21

belly. There are bound to be lots of fleas down there. Next, you need to find a smelly bone and hide it in your kennel. Cordelia will give you fresh bedding."

I left Dodger digging up a bone he'd buried in the onion patch, and went on around the town. I gave advice to anyone who needed it (and to some who said they didn't). Then I went home. The cleaning was finished, and Dr. Jeanie had a job for me.

"That dratted cat sneaked into the clinic again, Trump. Flush him out, will you? He must have a home to go to!"

She was talking about Major Higgins, of course. I am sure Higgins *does* have a home, but no one knows where it is. He's as sneaky as a cat can be and he operates on a "need to know" basis. One of these days I'll track him to his lair.

Dr. Jeanie let me into the clinic. I sniffed the air, then ran to the toy box in the corner and scraped it with my paw.

Dr. Jeanie tapped on the side of the box. "Time to go home, cat."

"That's *Major Higgins* to you, woman," muttered Higgins. He was curled up on a large teddy bear.

It was time to play the Enemies Game.

"Scat, cat." I lifted my lip to display my terrier teeth.

"Make me," said Higgins,

twitching his whiskers.

He yawned. I yapped. He hissed.
I snapped.

Higgins stood up and arched his
back, then stepped out of the box, a
paw at a time. He strolled towards
the door, muttering things I'd better
not repeat.

"Be off, cat," I said.

"In your dreams, dog." As he
waved his tail under my nose, I
sneezed.

Major Higgins and I are not
enemies. How could we be, when
he taught me how to use Cat-speak?
We just play the Enemies Game
to amuse Dr. Jeanie. Vets, just like
terriers, need to be entertained.

Trump's Diagnosis. If your dog is scratching a lot, it may have fleas. Fleas are insects that feed on dogs' blood. Their bites will make your dog cross and itchy, or even sick. Some dogs are allergic to fleabites. Oh, and don't forget: fleas like human blood too. If your dog has fleas, you need to wash the bedding as well as the dog.

Chapter 3

Thomasina

Vets need exercise to keep them happy and healthy. It is my duty to make sure Dr. Jeanie doesn't spend all her time at work. (This means playing Fetch the Frisbee is noble as well as fun.) One Thursday evening, I took Dr. Jeanie to Jeandabah Park. We had been playing for a while when a familiar voice called my name. "Trump! How's my favorite terrier-girl?"

I dropped the Frisbee and ran to meet Olivia Barnstormer. We used to see Olivia every week, when she brought her cat, Pusskin, to the clinic for his **injections.**

Injection (in-JECT-shn) – Medicine given with a hollow needle.

It was very sad when dear old Pusskin had to say goodnight forever.

Olivia bent and rubbed my ears, and I licked her hand.

"Did you contact Katya Gibbons about buying a kitten?" asked Dr. Jeanie. "She has a new litter."

"I'm not ready, yet," said Olivia. Her voice was bright, but to me it sounded like a Distress Call. "Next time, maybe," she said. I nosed her hand, and Olivia rubbed my head. "I know you mean to be kind, Jeanie, but Pusskin was special." She said goodbye, and we went back to our game.

Dr. Jeanie seemed sad, so I grabbed the Frisbee and pretended to run away. As I said, vets need their exercise.

When Dr. Jeanie and I got home, we were surprised to see Davie waiting on the porch.

I sniffed the air, with my tail in **query position**. I

> **Query Position –** Holding the tail out almost straight.

smelled Cat, but it wasn't Major Higgins, or any of the other cats I knew.

Davie stood on one leg. "Um, I've brought you a cat, Dr. Jeanie."

"I didn't know you had a pet, Davie," said Dr. Jeanie.

"Um, it's my auntie's cat," said Davie. He opened his jacket and showed us a **tortoiseshell** cat. It was small, skinny and scruffy, and it looked dazed. "He's hurt his head and his leg," Davie explained.

"Come into the clinic, Davie," said

Dr. Jeanie. She unlocked the door, and I led Davie into the examination room. Dr. Jeanie put on her white coat, and then laid a

Tortoiseshell
(TORT-iss-shell)
– A cat whose coat is a mixture of brown, black and orange hairs. They are almost always female.

fresh towel over the table. "Put Puss up here."

I jumped up on my special stool. It's set up in an alcove in the examination room so I can liaise with the patients without getting under Dr. Jeanie's feet. When Whiskey was A.L.O. he had a perch above the window.

"What's Puss's name?" asked Dr.

Jeanie.

"Um ... Tom," said Davie.

Dr. Jeanie smiled. "Really? This is a female cat, Davie. Tortoiseshell cats are almost always girls. Maybe it's short for Thomasina?"

"Maybe," said Davie. "He ... I mean, she fell off a fence and hurt her leg."

Dr. Jeanie listened to Thomasina's heart with her stethoscope, and then felt her all over. "You really did hurt yourself, little girl," she said.

Thomasina lay there like an old sock.

"She's bumped her head," said Dr. Jeanie. "This leg is broken, and there seems to be some swelling over her ribs." She frowned. "Davie, are you

31

sure she fell off a fence?"

"Um, yes. She was walking along a fence and she fell off it."

"Your aunt should have brought Thomasina in herself," said Dr. Jeanie. "She has quite serious injuries."

I heard Davie swallow. He moved over to me, and I put my nose into his hand. Sick animals are not the only ones who need comfort.

"Davie?" said Dr. Jeanie.

"Um, Auntie had to go and see her sister in the hospital," said Davie. "That's why she asked me to bring her to you. She would have come if she could, but she didn't want to miss her train. Can you fix Thomasina?"

"I ought to talk to your aunt first," said Dr. Jeanie, "but this leg needs to be set as soon as possible." She was gently feeling the cat's front leg. "It's a clean break, and should heal well."

"What about her head? She was knocked out."

"That's just a bruise, I think. We'll know more tomorrow." Dr. Jeanie smiled. "You'd better go on home now, Davie. Come around tomorrow afternoon with your aunt."

Davie closed his fingers gently around my nose and I licked his hand. I jumped off my stool and led Davie out of the clinic, wagging my tail to let him know everything would be all right. I hoped so, anyway.

When I got back, the light was on in the surgery room, so I knew Dr. Jeanie was going to set Thomasina's leg tonight.

If a broken bone is left to mend by itself, it might heal crooked. That's why vets, or doctors, set broken bones. Because Dr. Jeanie talks to herself while she's working, I know how she does it.

First, she sends the patient to sleep with something called **anesthetic**.

Then she puts the bone back the way it ought to go. Next, she uses

Anesthetic (an-ass-THET-ic) – A medicine that puts you to sleep or numbs pain.

special plaster bandages to hold
the bone in the proper place until
it has healed. This was what she
was doing for Thomasina. In a few
weeks, when the bone is mended,
Dr. Jeanie takes off the plaster.

I didn't go into the operating room, but I was waiting in the recovery ward when Thomasina woke up. Dr. Jeanie had put her in a warm bed in a cage so she wouldn't hurt herself again. I wrinkled my nose as I sat waiting for the patient to wake. I don't like the smell of **antiseptics** and anesthetic. They make me sneeze.

After a while, Dr. Jeanie looked in. She had been cleaning up the operating room.

"How is she, Trump?" she asked.

I wagged my tail to let her know

Antiseptic (ant-ee-SEP-tic) – Medicine that kills bacteria so wounds don't get infected.

everything was all right. Thomasina was still asleep, but she was starting to twitch her ears and one of her paws. I knew she would be awake soon.

Dr. Jeanie rubbed my ears. "There's something very strange about this case, Trump," she said.

Trump's Diagnosis. It is rare for a cat to fall off a fence. They have excellent balance and they can jump long distances. They usually land safely on their feet.

Chapter 4

cranky paws

Dr. Jeanie went through into
Cowfork House to make dinner.
I stayed in the recovery ward to
watch over Thomasina. Her ears
twitched, and her paws kept
moving. She made sad little mewing
sounds, and soon she opened her
eyes. I began my welcome speech.

"Hello, Thomasina," I said. "I
know you feel really bad just now.
You're scared, and you hurt, but you
will feel better very soon. Dr. Jeanie

has just –"

That was as far as I got, because Thomasina stopped looking dazy and hazy, and tried to leap away.

"Settle down!" I said. "Davie told us what happened, but –" I stopped, because Thomasina wasn't listening. She was muttering and mewing and making even less sense than sick cats usually do.

"No – no! Dog! Dog! Oh, help … no, please no – hurts – no –"

She scrabbled with her paws, and crammed herself into a corner of the cage.

"It's all right, Thomasina!" I said.

"Dog – dog – no – help … oh, it hurts –"

I realized that Thomasina was

afraid of dogs. Some cats are.

I backed away. "I won't hurt you," I said. "This is Pet Vet Clinic. I am a dog, but I'm also Dr. Jeanie's Animal Liaison Officer. You're quite safe with me."

Thomasina was trying to tie herself in knots, so I trotted through the door into Cowfork House. Dr. Jeanie was scrambling eggs in our kitchen. I love scrambled eggs, and I knew there would be a spoonful for me. I had to keep my mind on my job, though. I pushed my nose against Dr. Jeanie's leg, and then trotted back to the clinic.

Dr. Jeanie followed me, but when Thomasina saw her, she started scrabbling and crying again. "No

– no! Human! No, go away – no –"
She hissed and spat, and tried to
claw at Dr. Jeanie's hand.

"You're not a happy cat, are you,
Thomasina?" murmured Dr. Jeanie.
"We'll have our hands full with you.
Settle down, now. No one wants to
hurt you." She backed away, and
held out her hand to me. "Come
on, Trump. We'll leave Miss Cranky
Paws to herself."

Cranky Paws! I thought. That's a
good name for her.

We ate our scrambled eggs. Dr.
Jeanie had hers with toast, and I
had mine with kibble. After that,
Dr. Jeanie did some paperwork and
I snoozed. We went back to check
Cranky Paws twice, but she wasn't

pleased to see us.

We had Rounds the next morning, and when we came back, Davie was waiting. "How's, um – Thomasina?" he asked.

Dr. Jeanie frowned. "Not so good. Where's your aunt, Davie? I need to talk to her."

"She'll come when she gets back from the wedding," said Davie.

"I thought she'd gone to see her sister in the hospital," said Dr. Jeanie.

Davie stood on one leg. "Um …"

"Wherever she is, I need to see her about Thomasina," said Dr. Jeanie. "In the meantime, you go in. She might calm down when she sees someone familiar."

I led Davie to the recovery ward

while Dr. Jeanie prepared for the afternoon clinic.

Cranky Paws was still not pleased to see me. She didn't want to see Davie, either. She spat and hissed at both of us.

"Not happy, is she?" asked Dr. Jeanie as she buttoned her white coat. "I have to give her a pill. Will she let you hold her, Davie?"

Davie stretched his hand towards the cage. Thomasina wailed a warning, then spat. Davie backed away.

"Is she always this cranky?" asked Dr. Jeanie.

"I don't really know," said Davie. "Um – Auntie Mel hasn't had her very long."

Before Dr. Jeanie could ask any more questions, we heard the bell tinkle as someone opened the clinic door. The first patient had arrived.

Davie left, and I went to help Dr. Jeanie. That's one problem with working in a busy place like Pet Vet Clinic. All the patients and their people need help and attention, so we have to decide who needs it most, and when.

Should I spend my time with Cranky Paws, or should I be with the scared puppy who had come in for his **vaccination?** I chose the puppy,

> **Vaccination**
> (Vax-in-AISH-n)
> — Medicine given, mostly by injection, to prevent illness.

because he whined for me to come. He didn't like the smell in the examining room, and he missed his dog mother. After his injection, I washed his face and we played a little game of pounce-paw while his person talked to Dr. Jeanie.

Trump's diagnosis. Nervous puppies need you to be calm and friendly. If you comfort them too much when they're scared, they think you're scared too. Playing a little game sometimes takes their minds off things.

Major Higgins
to the Rescue?

When the puppy had gone, Dodger
came in with Cordelia. I noticed he
smelled of flea soap. Cordelia had
come to ask Dr. Jeanie if she could
buy flea soap that smelled of roses.
Dr. Jeanie said no, she couldn't. She
gave Dodger something to fix the
sore patch he'd chewed on his flank.

"I did just as you said, and Cordelia
washed my bedding," Dodger told me.
"You are clever, Trump."

Next, Primrose the Persian came in to have her teeth cleaned, and then it was a poodle named Jazz who had had a fight with a bicycle.

After Dr. Jeanie had stitched the poodle's sore shoulder, I noticed Major Higgins gliding in through the clinic window.

"I thought that window was closed," I said when I cornered him by the leash display.

Higgins fluffed his whisker-cushions at me. "A capable agent can infiltrate any enemy position unseen." (Higgins often talks like that. He has a military mind.)

"I need some advice," I said.

"It'll cost you." Higgins flipped his tail.

"It's to help a fellow feline."

"Oh," said Higgins. "Is she cute?"

I ignored that. "It's a tortoiseshell named Cranky Paws."

"Cranky Paws?"

"Her name is Thomasina, really. She has a broken leg and bruising, from falling off a fence."

"That's not a likely story," said Higgins. "Cats don't fall off fences."

"Davie said this one did," I said. "Anyway, she's upset and cranky. How can I get her to listen to me?"

"You can't," said Higgins. "You're a dog." He flicked his tail.

"I am an A.L.O. first and a dog second," I reminded him. "If she won't listen to me, she might listen to you. Tell her that the sooner she calms down, the sooner she can go

49

back where she came from. If she
keeps panicking, she'll hurt her leg
again."

I thought Higgins would say
something sarcastic, but he just
preened his whiskers. "Thomasina,
you say? A trim little tortoiseshell?"

"She's in the recovery ward in a
hospital cage."

"Leave it to me. Major Higgins
to the rescue." Higgins glanced
over my shoulder and peered hard
at something behind me. I turned
to see what he was staring at, and
when I looked back, he was gone.

I went to the door to greet the
next patient, a guinea pig with a
sore eye. Guinea pigs have little to
say apart from "food!" or "breed!",

but I did my best. I was watching
Dr. Jeanie putting ointment in the
guinea pig's eye when I heard a
shriek from the recovery ward. A
few seconds later, Higgins shot
out. He was halfway through the
window before I could stop him,
so I darted out the back door and
intercepted him on the other side.

"What did you do to Cranky Paws?" I asked.

"Nothing!" huffed Higgins. "Look what *she* did to *me*!" He showed me a scratch on his nose. "I spoke to her like a father. I was reassuring and kindly."

"Why did she claw you, then?"

"I was telling her how she could go back where she came from as soon as she started behaving like a sensible cat, and she went crazy."

He puffed out his whisker-cushions and squinted at his nose. "She's a feisty feline, Trump. If she'd launch a missile strike at a major of the **clowder**, there's no

> **Clowder**
> (CLOUD-er) – A group of cats.

knowing what she'd do to a mere dog. This cat has serious problems."

"Can you find out why she went crazy?" I asked.

Higgins hesitated. "I could, but I won't. I have too much respect for my nose." He scanned the area and slipped away.

Trump's diagnosis. When animals are afraid, they usually run away. If they can't run, they might attack. Not all cats are afraid of dogs. Cats and dogs that grow up together will probably be friends. If you bring a puppy or a kitten to a home that has a grown-up dog or cat, you need to introduce them carefully.

The Very Busy Auntie

When Davie came to work on Saturday, Dr. Jeanie asked if his aunt was back from the wedding.

"What w – oh, yes, she did come back, but now she's in Italy," said Davie.

Dr. Jeanie stared. "What did she say when you told her I'd set Thomasina's leg?"

"She said thanks." Davie began to take bedding out of one of the hospital cages.

Cranky Paws had been crouching in the corner of her cage. She tried to claw her way through the mesh when she saw Davie.

"Humans – ow! No, no, no!" she muttered.

I moved slowly forward and sat up on my hind legs so she could see me. "Thomasina … it's Davie. You know Davie. He's your friend. He brought you here."

Thomasina pinned her ears back and glared at me.

"Is she any better?" Davie asked.

"I think she'll be all right," said Dr. Jeanie. "It's a real struggle to get any **medication** into her, though. I wish your aunt could make time to come in."

"She's really busy," said Davie. He looked over at Cranky Paws.

"Give me your aunt's

> **Medication**
> (med-i-KAY-shn) – Medicine. Something to help cure or ease sickness.

details when you finish there," said Dr. Jeanie.

Davie washed the bedding and then came back to scrub the cages. As usual, the smell of disinfectant made me sneeze, but there were no Distress Calls, so I didn't go out. I could tell Davie was feeling bad. So was Dr. Jeanie. Even Higgins was sulking over his scratched nose. It was time for me to speak firmly with the patient.

My chance came when Dr. Jeanie moved Cranky Paws' cage onto the porch, away from the noise. "Keep an eye on her, Trump," she said.

I sat a little way from the cage. Cranky Paws muttered and hissed and glowered at me through slitted eyes.

"You can hate me all you like," I said to her, "but I am an A.L.O. I have a job to do. Dr. Jeanie asked me to look after you." I sat up a bit straighter so she could see I meant business. "You must be feeling better by now," I said.

Cranky Paws' ears clamped down and her tail began to lash.

"A bit of gratitude would be good," I said. "I know you're hurt,

but I've seen animals much worse
off than you. There was a cat who
was very old and very sick. Dr.
Jeanie gave him injections that hurt
him, but he still managed to purr for
her."

I could tell I wasn't getting
through to Cranky Paws.

"What did you scratch Higgins
for? He was trying to help you. So

am I. So is Dr. Jeanie. Don't you get it, cat? *Everyone* is trying to help you so you can go home. Why –"

"Wrowwwwww!" *Spoing!* Cranky Paws tried to claw her way out of the cage.

"All right, all *right*!" I said. "Just pretend I'm not here."

I was glad when Dr. Jeanie came to fetch Cranky Paws back into the hospital after the cleaning was done. I had been rather proud of my work as Dr. Jeanie's A.L.O., but now I felt like a failure.

Dr. Jeanie took Davie back into the clinic to fill out Cranky Paws' details. Vets keep files on their patients so they have records of all sorts of things. They know when patients have their vaccinations, and what illnesses or injuries they've had. They know what treatments were used, and how well they worked. Each file begins with the animal's breed, name and age, and the owner's name and contact details. These were the things Dr. Jeanie needed from Davie.

"Thomasina is a tortoiseshell cat around three years old," said Dr. Jeanie. "You said your aunt hadn't had her long, Davie. Do you have any idea where she got her?"

"Not really," said Davie. I noticed he was standing on one leg again.

"I need your aunt's name, address and contact details," Dr. Jeanie went on.

"Auntie Mel lives in Cobber Street. It's a white house near the end."

"And what is Auntie Mel's last name?"

"Um, Raymond, like mine."

"So, her full name is Melanie Raymond. Telephone number?"

"I can't remember," said Davie. He changed legs and peered out the window.

Dr. Jeanie sighed. "I'll fill in those details later. Off you go, Davie, and *please* tell your auntie to get in touch with me."

Davie went home, and Dr. Jeanie finished her paperwork. "Trump, I think our Saturday helper is hiding something. I don't think his auntie really *is* in Italy."

I pushed my nose into Dr. Jeanie's hand. I was *sure* he was hiding something. So was Cranky Paws Thomasina.

Trump's diagnosis. Part of being a vet is reading body language. Dogs use body language a lot. So do cats and people. If people don't look at you, they might be hiding something. If dogs *do* look at you they might be waiting to see what you will do, or they might be making a challenge.

Chapter 7

The Truth aBout Cranky Paws

On Sunday morning, Dr. Jeanie
and I went for a walk. I wasn't a bit
surprised to find we were heading
for Cobber Street.

"There can't be too many white
houses with people called Mel
Raymond living in them," said Dr.
Jeanie. She was right. We found the
place in just a few minutes.

I stood up on my hind legs to
look over the garden wall. Inside,
the garden was overgrown and

untidy. I sniffed several times.
I could smell sparrows and
blackbirds, but no cats.

Dr. Jeanie opened the gate and
we walked up the garden path to
ring the doorbell. I sniffed again, but
there wasn't so much as a whiff of
Cranky Paws.

I was still puzzling over that
when Davie's Auntie Mel opened
the door.

"Yes?" she said. She had a nice
voice, so I wagged my tail – a proper
wag, all the way from root to tip.

"Hello," said Dr. Jeanie. "I'm
sorry to bother you, but it's about
Thomasina."

Auntie Mel looked surprised.
"I'm sorry?"

"I'm from Pet Vet Clinic," said Dr. Jeanie.

"Ah!" said Davie's aunt. "You must be Dr. Jeanie, the vet my nephew works for."

"We're in the right place, then, if you're Miss Raymond."

"Call me Mel." She clicked her

fingers to me. "I wish I could have a dog like yours, but I'm away from home a lot."

"So we heard," said Dr. Jeanie. "I hope your sister is better."

Mel smiled. "I don't have a sister. Davie's dad is my brother."

"But you have been to a wedding?" said Dr. Jeanie.

"Not lately, no," said Davie's aunt, laughing.

"Italy?"

"Yes. You know, Dr. Jeanie, I have no idea what's going on. I've been working in Italy for six months. Davie wrote and told me all about his job, but I just flew home last night. I'm a bit **jetlagged**.

"Why don't you come in and explain?"

Mel gave Dr. Jeanie some coffee, and found a plain

Jetlag (JET-lag) – A sleepy feeling caused by traveling through different time zones.

biscuit for me. Then we tried to work out what was going on.

"I can't imagine why Davie told you all those fibs about hospitals and weddings," said Mel. "He knew perfectly well I was in Italy all the time."

"So, Thomasina is not your cat?" said Dr. Jeanie.

"I haven't had a cat for years. I love animals, but it isn't fair to have pets if you can't give them plenty of attention."

I knew Mel was telling the truth. My nose would have known if Cranky Paws had lived here.

"We've disturbed your Sunday for nothing, then," said Dr. Jeanie. "But Davie did say Thomasina belonged to his Auntie Mel Raymond who lived in Cobber Street."

"I'll have a word with young Davie," said Mel, as we left for home.

"So will I," said Dr. Jeanie to me.

❖

"We met your aunt today, Davie," said Dr. Jeanie, when Davie came to see Cranky Paws that afternoon.

"And we didn't have to go to Italy to do it."

Davie took a couple of steps backwards, and stood on one leg. "I suppose you're mad at me."

"I'm not pleased," said Dr. Jeanie. "It seems I've been treating a completely strange cat. I have no idea who owns her, and I expect they're worried sick about where she is!"

"No, they're not!" Davie had been staring at his toes, but now he swung his head up, and almost overbalanced.

"Tell me," said Dr. Jeanie. "And Davie? Make it the truth this time."

The story Davie told us explained

a lot about Cranky Paws. It explained why she was afraid of people, and why she was so **malnourished**.

> **Malnourished**
> (mal-NURR-ish-d)
> – Thin from not getting enough good food.

Cranky Paws didn't want to go back where she came from, and who could blame her?

"I took the train down to the city on Thursday," said Davie. "I saw some boys kicking a can around. One of them kicked it into a corner near some trash bins, and a cat rushed out." He looked up at Dr. Jeanie, and then down at me. I put my nose into his hand.

"Go on," said Dr. Jeanie.

"It was her – Thomasina, I mean. She must have thought the boy was trying to hit her, because she shot right across the street and into a bicycle."

Davie bent and picked me up and I pushed my nose under his chin.

"What did you do?" asked Dr. Jeanie.

"I went to see if the rider was all right, and then I saw Thomasina was running off on three legs. I went after her, and she wobbled and fell over. I was going to take her to her owner, but the boys said not to bother. She was just a stray. One of them said the people who owned her had moved away and left her. That's when I decided to bring her to you."

"That explains the injuries," said Dr. Jeanie. "It also explains why she's malnourished and **feral**. But why did you make up that tall tale about your aunt and the hospital and the wedding? Why not just tell the truth?"

> **Feral** (FERR-al) – A domestic animal that has gone wild.

"Dunno," muttered Davie. "I was worried you'd only help her if you thought she had an owner who could, um, pay for her operation."

"Didn't you realize I might have had some unkind thoughts about your Auntie Mel? I know a neglected cat when I see one, and Thomasina has been badly neglected."

"I'm sorry," said Davie. "I suppose you don't want me to work for you anymore."

"Of course I do!" said Dr. Jeanie. She shook her head at Davie. "You're a silly boy, but your heart's in the right place. Can you give her a home when she's well?"

Davie looked miserable. "I wish I could, but our landlord won't let us have animals. And Auntie Mel keeps going away."

"In that case," said Dr. Jeanie, "we really have a problem."

Trump's diagnosis. Some people leave cats behind when they move away. They think cats can live by hunting rats and mice. This is cruel and thoughtless.

No More
Miss Cranky Paws

Dr. Jeanie was right. Finding a home
for a cat like Cranky Paws wasn't
going to be easy. Most people who
want a cat get a cute kitten. Cranky
Paws wasn't a kitten. She wasn't
even a nice cat.

I gave the problem some thought,
chewing it over while I chewed my
Sunday beef bone. Maybe I needed
a game of Fetch the Frisbee to clear
my mind?

Thinking about that gave me an idea.

I hid the bone under the step, and went to visit Cranky Paws. She spat when she saw me, but she had eaten her food.

I sat in front of the cage. "Cranky Paws?" I said. "I have to talk to you, and you have to listen."

"Go away, dog. And don't call me nasty names."

I started again. "I'll call you Thomasina, then. Would you like a new home, Thomasina, with someone who will never go away and leave you?"

Cranky Paws flickered her ears. For the first time, I thought she was listening.

"Would there be fish?" she asked.

"Probably. You would be with people –"

Her ears went back and she hissed. "I hate people. People hurt."

"Stop that," I said. "Most people are nice to cats if cats are nice to them. Spitting and scratching is not being nice."

Thomasina didn't answer.

"Here's the deal," I said. "I will organize a new home for you, but it means no more Miss Cranky Paws. Get that, Thomasina?"

"Dogs don't organize homes for cats," said Thomasina.

"I am Dr. Jeanie's A.L.O.," I said. "I can do it, but you have to do as I say. If a nice human comes up to your cage, you have to mew, and you have to keep your claws to yourself. You might even purr – if you can. Deal?"

"Pfft!" said Thomasina. "You can't do it. Nobody wants me."

"Somebody needs you though," I said, and I went to make things happen for Thomasina.

I ran up Cobber Street, but I wasn't going to visit Mel. I turned right and headed into Pippin Road, where Olivia Barnstormer lives.

Olivia was in her garden, pulling weeds. I barked several times. I used my urgent bark – the one that lets people know that something needs attention.

"Trump!" Olivia tried to pat me, but I dodged out of reach. "What are you doing here? Where's Jeanie?"

I pranced my paws and barked again, then darted back out her gate.

Olivia put her gardening gloves in the wheelbarrow.

I dashed and darted again. I wanted her to follow me back to Pet Vet Clinic, but she went into the house and telephoned Dr. Jeanie.

I heard half the conversation through the window.

"Jeanie, your Trump is here. I'm not sure what she wants. She's acting oddly."

Pause.

"Well, yes ... if I can catch her. See you soon."

A little bit later, Olivia came out again. I went up to her and sat in good-dog position while she tied a rope to my collar. Then I led her back to Pet Vet and around the back to the clinic.

I took her up to Cranky Paws'
cage. Then I sat down and crossed
my paws and hoped.

Cranky Paws saw me and her ears
went back.

"*Don't!*" I said. "This person
is good to cats. She would never
abandon you."

Cranky Paws swished her
whiskers back and forth, and then
she managed a mew.

Olivia looked down at her.
"Who's this?" She read the name on
Cranky Paws' cage. "Thomasina?"

I heard Dr. Jeanie come in.
"Trump, you naughty girl! What do
you mean by bothering Olivia like
that?"

Olivia undid the rope from my collar, then reached out a finger to Cranky Paws. Dr. Jeanie made a move to stop her, but the cat carefully wiped her whiskers along Olivia's finger.

"Well, well," said Dr. Jeanie softly. "Olivia, you're the very first person that cat hasn't tried to attack!"

Olivia turned back. "I hope she doesn't attack her owner."

"She doesn't have one." Dr. Jeanie must have had the same idea I had, because she started moving around the room, tidying a few things. As she tidied, she told Olivia what Davie had told us.

"Unfortunately, Davie can't give her a home," said Dr. Jeanie.

"I suppose *I* could take her," said Olivia.

"She's basically healthy, and her injuries are healing well, but it's only fair to tell you she's a cranky, standoffish creature."

"That would suit me, I think," said Olivia. "No cat could ever take Pusskin's place. That's why I felt it would be unfair to take in a kitten. But Thomasina needs a home." She put out her finger again. Cranky Paws did another whisker wipe. And then we heard a peculiar buzzing sound …

Cranky Paws was purring.

I wagged my tail and Dr. Jeanie
smiled. Helping animals and their
people is the best job in the world.

Trump's diagnosis. People who have lost a pet don't always want another one right away, but sometimes sad animals and sad people can help one another not to be sad anymore.

About the Authors

Darrel and Sally Odgers live in Tasmania with their Jack Russell terriers, Tess, Trump, Jeanie and Preacher, who compete to take them for walks. They enjoy walks, because that's when they plan their stories. They toss ideas around and pick the best. They are also the authors of the popular *Jack Russell: Dog Detective* series.

Also By Darrel and Sally Odgers

JACK RUSSELL: Dog Detective

Jack Russell:
the detective with
a nose for crime.